Náidin's Song:
Twins
A Novella in the Náidin's Song Cycle

I0518680

J'nae Rae Spano

Colony Creators Press

Náidin's Song: Twins
First Edition
© 2020 J'nae Rae Spano.

Cover Design: Graphicfantastic.com

ISBN- 978-0-9979645-5-4

CONTENTS

Acknowledgments

Thank you to my writer's group the Penny Dreadfuls for all your help in bringing this story to life. I couldn't have done it without your support. Thank you to my husband, Chris, for allowing me the time to work on it and the D&D game that sparked it. Thank you to all my beta readers who encouraged me...And a special dedication to my departed best friend, Jeanne Whistler, who wanted to see Kalidin's story and lives on in the story as Díja.

CHAPTER 1:
KALIDIN'S 1ST VERSE

Today was Winter Tide, the day of their birth. Moreover, it was their tenth annual; their Name Day. No longer could they be called by their baby names.

The elder twin sat on his bed across from the younger. His brother, of all days to be caught in a Dreaming, was still fast asleep. He looked around the room full of the trappings of childhood. Toys, puzzles, and games lined the shelves only half-visible in the gloom of the light filtered through the slatted shutters.

He would miss their home and parents. He supposed every dwarfling did. But, unlike the others, he'd have his twin.

He sniffed at the air; the smells of the kitchen were absent this morning. "Right, fasting," he huffed. Not fair, considering the Earthen Folk celebrated Winter Tide with feasts beginning at sunrise.

He heard a short rap on the door before his parents entered. He smiled at them. "Good morning, Father, Mother."

His father nodded and frowned when he saw his brother still sleeping. "Meráda, I'll carry the boy to the bathhouse. Hopefully, he'll wake before he's presented."

His mother nodded and held out her hand. "Come, my son."

He slid from his bed and jammed his feet into his slippers as she pulled him up. "Yes, Mother."

He followed close behind his father, his mother's hand between his shoulder blades a constant gentle nudge forward.

Steam billowed out the bathhouse door like fog rolling into the valley, the damp air a heavy warm blanket, scented with evergreen oils. He kicked off his slippers as he shed his night and small clothes, before easing into the fragrant hot water.

His parents stripped his brother and lowered him into the shallow seat alcove in the bath. His twin sighed and curled up into his side.

He positioned himself to support his brother's head above the water. His brother's lids fluttered open, his pupils dilated from the vestige of his Dreaming. He rubbed his brother's back. "What did you see?"

His twin shook his head. "Doesn't make sense."

"Enough talking, boys." Their mother's stern tone left little room for complaint. "Wash."

He gave his sleepy brother a push then reached for the soap and brush. Something in his parent's demeanor bothered him. He strained his ears as the door closed behind them.

"You saw? … youngest …ill … brother. How … do … tell the elder … twin … be dead … forbidden … speak … ter today?"

He could hear the despair in his mother's voice as his mind raced to fill in the missing words.

"We don't." His father's voice carried better. "He'll know when the Priests sever their bond. Even he knows as of sunrise today, it is forbidden to address or refer to them by their baby names."

His heart beat hard against his breastbone hearing his father's words.

"So … don't … younger … not get … name? We let … choose … Temple or …ile?"

He looked over at his twin to find him floating on his back in the steaming water, oblivious to the conversation on the other side of the door.

His mother continued though her crying masked her words. He crawled out of the bath and crept to the door.

"I suppose we are." His father's voice lowered, "You … let … take …

birth."

He pressed his ear to the door as his mother replied. "I couldn't. Not when my Dreamings tell me our sons' names will be known throughout the world."

Names. Mother's Dreamings indicated their names. He sighed in relief. He wished he had Dreamings that guided him. His twin seemed to have inherited the ones meant for him as well.

"I know, as have I. It is why I have denied them every time they've tried to take him since his Dreamings started. Meráda, we must trust in the Dreamings we've been sent."

He turned to see his brother staring at him, an eyebrow raised. He shook his head and rejoined his twin in the water. Should he worry his brother with what he'd heard? Or trust his mother's Dreamings?

He pulled the gray woven spider silk and rabbit hair trousers on. "Mother, these are a bit tight," he complained.

His mother looked up from braiding his brother's hair. "They'll do for today, you won't need them after."

He huffed. "Why not?"

"You will wear school robes," his father replied as he draped a sapphire blue silk sash bordered in a silver geometric pattern. The area at his hip held the crest of House Nerhaed, embroidered with gold, silver, and copper thread.

He fingered the edge of the sash. It went well with the emerald green spider silk tunic.

"Wear it proudly, you are the Elder son in the Second Line," his father said as he squeezed his shoulder.

His brother fingered the silver and copper border on his own sash.

His stomach grumbled as they made their way to the mountain halls. The smells of the bonfires and roasting meat wafted up from the river valley, making him more aware of the festivities they were missing. No celebration delayed one's name day. Not even one as important and grand as Winter Tide.

His brother trudged alongside, his brow knit in concentration. A clear sign he mulled over his latest Dreaming. He wished he'd discuss it with him. He flicked his brother in the back of his head.

"Ow," his twin glared over at him as he retaliated by punching him in the arm.

"You going to tell me what is going on in that head of yours?"

He shook his head. "Not now. When our naming is done."

They followed their parents into the Temple area. Lord Gríson wasn't present to give them their lesson. A Priest of Cyríon met them at the door instead.

"Come boys," the Priest beckoned and led them from their parents and to a contemplation pool. "Nerhaed House consecrates the younger twin to the Temple." The Priest urged them to their knees, a hand on their heads. "Lord Gríson made his wish known to uphold the tradition. You have reached your naming day, and the choice to follow the tradition belongs to you. Either or both of you could offer yourself to the Body of Cyríon and never take a name. You also can both choose to ignore your House's tradition."

A gentle smile graced his twin's face. "It is not my calling, nor Cyríon's will."

The calmness his twin spoke with made his heart soar with pride. True, he could take his brothers place and satisfy Lord Gríson's sense of honor. However, lacking the Dreamings, he felt apart from his people. He could not become part of that which he had no affinity.

"Sit here and think on your futures until you are called to the Grande Hall for your Namings. The Priest left them.

Once the Priest's footsteps faded away, he heard his twin snort as he elbowed him. "I have a better idea than staring at a pool on our knees all day."

He turned to look at his brother. "What?"

"The inner lake."

He followed his twin down the winding crevasses that lead to the deep subterranean lake. His brother found it when they'd been gathered in the mountain for the Feast of Cyríon. Soon they'd be too big to squeeze through. "We shouldn't be doing this."

"Shush," his twin hissed, "They'll find us by the echo."

He sighed. There was no dissuading his twin when he wanted to do something.

They made their way by feel as the light faded. Blue flashes of bioluminescent light lit the end of their trail as water dripped into the lake.

His brother picked up a flat stone and flicked across the surface of the water, setting off multiple explosions of light. After he watched his brother skip a few more stones across the lake, he shrugged and joined him.

CHAPTER 2:
NÁIDIN'S 1ST VERSE

"Run, we can't be late!" He looked over his shoulder and beckoned his brother, before racing off through the halls. They would be in serious trouble if they arrived after sunset; it was their Naming Ceremony after all.

The other shook his head and groaned. "It was your idea to skip stones on the lake and now you're in a hurry?" The elder twin sprinted after him.

"You didn't have to agree." Skidding to a halt, he turned and made a face at his brother. His twin stumbled as he burst out laughing.

Their mother grabbed hold of her laughing child's arm. "By Cyríon, what is with you two? Of all days to choose to find mischief!"

This ended his brother's laughter, whose arm was caught in her strong grip. "Sorry, Mother."

He gulped, expecting a reprimand. No one had spoken their baby names all day, which had given him the wicked idea of running off for fun before the ceremony. No one could call them back as they had no names since sunrise.

"Do you wish the dishonor of being nameless until your next birthing day?" She looked at them, her brows knit in disapproval.

"No, Mother." He bowed his head. "We lost track of time."

Their mother's face softened into a smile as she looked them over. "At least you remain presentable." She slipped her hand down his brother's arm to clasp his hand as she captured his own in the other. "Stand straight, heads up." She led them to the archway to the Grande Hall.

Their father, Thalin, stood before Lord Gríson, the head of Nerhaed House. His sigh of relief at seeing his sons visible even at a distance. Their father turned and bowed his head. "Milord, I present to you my sons, who on this day have reached the tenth annual of their birth."

"Twins are rare, Cousin." Lord Gríson tapped their father to rise. "For both to survive to their naming rarer still."

He turned to the opening where his sons and wife waited. "Meráda, bring them forward."

She nodded. Keeping hold of their hands, she brought them before Lord Gríson. She nudged her eldest forward.

He took a step forward and knelt before the head of their House with his face raised up.

Lord Gríson tapped the dwarfling's forehead. "From this moment forward, you are Kalidin, Son of Thalin of Nerhaed House."

Kalidin bowed his head once he received his name. "I thank you, Milord, for giving me the honor of a name."

"Rise and stand behind me."

Kalidin did as instructed. As he turned around, he smiled as the younger felt his mother nudge him forward.

He followed his brother's example.

Lord Gríson looked down at him as he met the gaze of the Head of his House. He remained silent under the Lord's scrutiny. The pause caused nervous side-glances between their parents. Kalidin's smile faded as he watched him continue to kneel, awaiting his name.

"It is not often, one gives a name to both twins. It is said twins are harbingers of change, whether it be for good or ill, one often wonders. It was not I who received the Dreaming for your name young one, only your brother's was given me. It was the King to whom your name was revealed. Had it been any other, I would reject it and give you the choice of entering the Temple or be cast out, nameless. Before I give it, I ask you to honor our House's tradition and enter the Priesthood of your own volition."

He resisted looking away. To allow the fact his name was not given to his House's Lord to bring him shame would be to reject it. To refuse a name or be unworthy of one meant exile, the only option his Dreaming left him.

He raised his chin higher in defiance his gaze locked eye to eye with Lord Gríson. "It is not my calling, Milord. My Dreamings forbid it."

As the sunset chimes began, the Lord sighed. He reached out a hand and tapped his forehead as he had his brother's. "From this moment forward, you are Náidin, Son of Thalin of Nerhaed House."

Náidin bowed his head, relief washing over him. "I thank you, Milord, for giving me the honor of a name."

"Rise and join your brother. You both leave your parents' house for the Halls of Learning. You may have a moment with them," He gestured to the door opposite where they'd entered, "afterwards you both go through that door." He stalked out of the Grande Hall.

Náidin looked to his parents. "I am sorry. I almost brought dishonor on our family."

His father placed a hand on his shoulder. "My esteemed cousin has a quarrel with me. You held your head high; it was he who tried to bring dishonor, not you, Náidin," his father smiled saying his son's name for the first time. "I couldn't be prouder of you and Kalidin. My sons."

Náidin felt his brother's arm wrap around his shoulders. He snaked his own around his brother's waist. "I'll miss you Mother, Father."

Kalidin nodded. "We both will."

Their mother put a hand on their shoulders. "We will miss you too. I am with your Father, I couldn't be prouder of the two of you."

"This is not the last we'll see of you today. The Winter Tide Starlight Feast is tonight. Consigned to the Halls doesn't keep you from your family on the festivals." He ruffled both their heads. "Now go, get settled. We'll see you at the bonfire."

The twins followed the corridor to the Halls of Learning. The passage opened into a chamber with many doors, one of which stood open. They continued through the open door down a short hall that opened into a reception area. They approached the desk of their Ten Year House Mother. She looked up from her papers and regarded them with blue eyes. "Bless my eyes!" She winked at them, her voice full of warmth and mirth, "Am I seeing double?"

"No Mistress." Náidin bowed. "I am Náidin, Son of Thalin of House Nerhaed."

His brother followed suit. "I am Kalidin, Son of Thalin of House Nerhaed."

"Welcome young Masters, I'm House Mother Díja." She placed two sets of clothes and bedding in front of them. "Go change to your uniforms. Your dormitory is through the door to the left. Pick from the unclaimed beds."

"Yes, Mistress." Kalidin took the bundles, handing half to Náidin.

"Tonight we join the feast of the Winter Tide festival. The other students are spending the day with their kin. After tomorrow's fast for the Day of Introspect, all your meals will be taken in the school's refectory, other than the festivals. You will join your families on such days. You, however, will wear only your uniforms until you are released to apprentice in your chosen trades when your Ten Year concludes." She looked at their finery. "Your family is highly placed in their House. On Cyríon's Feast Day, you will wear your family's colors and your sashes for all other festivals.

"Yes, Mistress Díja," they answered.

Náidin followed close behind Kalidin. His stomach roiled now that his trial was over. His Dreamings said he could not choose to pledge to the Temple. It took the fear of exile to not look away.

He glanced around the room of six bunks. Two of the top mattresses had no bedding one was to the left as they entered; the other was at the back on the right. Náidin bit his lip.

Kalidin dropped his uniforms in the first open chest and climbed up to make his bed. Náidin bowed his head and shuffled to the back. *Too far.* He sighed as he took the last bunk.

His bunk made, he stripped out of his best clothes and changed into the uniform his House sash draped over it. The heavy course wool made him itch.

He closed his eyes and smiled as his brother tugged his hair. "Thank you, Kal, uhm Kalidin."

"When I finish removing your braid, you can do mine." Kalidin chuckled. "If you want, you can call me Kal.

"Huh? Oh, I'm not used to our names." He tugged at his sleeve. "I think I like Kal, though."

"Stop fidgeting, Ná!"

Náidin wrinkled his nose. "Sounds more like you're making a pony sound." He snorted. "Let's not shorten mine."

Kalidin leaned against his brother laughing. "True."

"Shall I remove yours now?"

"Aye."

"Well then, let go." He shrugged out of Kalidin's hug and moved behind to undo the braid down his brother's back. His hands shook as he unwound the plait.

"Náidin, are you well?"

"Aye. I feared I wouldn't get my name." He combed out Kalidin's hair with his trembling fingers. "There."

"I would have gone into exile with you."

"I wouldn't have let you," he whispered.

"We should go to the Bonfire now." Kalidin gave Náidin a shove towards the door. "After having to fast for our naming, I'm starved."

"I don't think I can eat," Náidin shuffled out the door, his brother following behind him. *Cyríon, comfort my soul and guide me.*

His twin caught up beside him and draped his arm over his shoulders.

Náidin gave Kalidin a half-smile as he wrapped his arm around his brother's waist. A sense of peace settled over him after the stress-filled day. He took a deep breath and let it out slow.

Díja waited in the Grande Hall for them."Let's get you to your House table, shall we?" There was a jounce in her step as she headed towards the exit.

Náidin felt at ease with the round House Mother. She seemed to walk to the rhythm of a song only she could hear. Her tight curls bounced ever so slightly as she bobbed her head. He felt his own feet pick up the cadence she set, causing Kalidin to stumble as they walked arm-n-arm.

"Sorry." Náidin bit his lip as he held back laughter.

"No. You are not." Kalidin disengaged and swatted him on the back of the head.

Soon they were out in the snow and trudging down the path to the valley. Their breath coalesced in the chill air. The moon shone bright in the clear sky, and the arc of the ring cut a swath through luminous stars.

Díja stopped at a clearing near the last stair. "I will wait for everyone here, once the Feast ends."

"Yes, Mistress," the brothers replied.

Náidin reached for another roll to sop up the gravy on his plate. His stomach felt as if he'd been feasting all day rather than fasting, and still, he stuffed himself more. He'd more than found his appetite once the smells of roasted meat met his nose.

Kalidin elbowed him in the ribs. "You'll give yourself a stomachache."

He looked over at his twin's plate, with the remnants of his meal. "Have to make up for missing the earlier meals." He stuffed the soaked bread into his mouth.

Lord Gríson sat down across from the twins, next to their father. His cold stare succeeded where Kalidin's rebuke had not. Náidin set the half-eaten roll on his plate and pushed it away.

"Named or no, you can still choose to honor our House tradition when you choose your vocation in ten annuals, or preferably in five rather than exploring the trades" the terseness of his tone made Náidin cringe.

"Am I to deny Cyríon's will then?"

"Presumptuous child."

"Leave him be, Cousin," Thalin glared at Lord Gríson, "House traditions are not laws writ in stone."

"Traditions bring order," Lord Gríson said, banging his fist on the table. "And your family defies my will. Am I not the keeper of our House interests?"

"Of what interest is forcing Náidin to the priesthood?" Meráda asked.

"I promised him to the Body of Cyríon once it was known you carried twins," he glared at Meráda. "I have already lost honor in the fact he is now named. The best I can hope for is that he serves as Priest to care for those, part of the Body."

"That sect loses more favor as the years pass. It is nothing more than a cult that enslaves babies to constant Dreamings." Meráda stood up, her hands on her hips.

"Thalin, I warned you against wedding this heretic."

"Leave my mother alone," Náidin shot to his feet. "It is not Cyríon's will I serve him as part of his Body, nor as a Priest. I will let him guide me where he will, as I serve him; not you, Milord."

Gríson eyes narrowed. "How do you serve him, Child?"

"By honoring the Dreamings he sends me. He forbad me to choose the

Priesthood. Had you refused to bestow the name I was given, I would've trusted him to protect me in my exile." Náidin blinked back tears.

"As long as you remain outside the Temple, I will not condone any choice you make. You are, in fact, sanctioned for refusing my will." Lord Gríson held out his hand. "Hand me your sash."

Náidin frowned. "I don't understand."

"And me?" Kalidin asked.

"As long as you uphold our traditions, you are spared your twin's sanction."

"But what does it mean, Milord?" Náidin pleaded his fingers tracing the edge of his new sash.

"It means exactly what I said, Child. You do not have the support of my House in any path you take, outside the Temple."

"I have been taught that our Dreamings are sacred gifts, not to be ignored. How can I follow your will when it is against Cyríon's? Are not our Dreamings from him?"

The Priest who met them earlier approached the table. "The child is correct, Lord Gríson. If his Dreamings forbid it, he would be amiss in choosing to enter the Temple.

"Did you not assure me, he was meant for Cyríon's service?"

"Náidin is. I am more certain of it now that his name is known. One so named is in the Dreamings of the Temple. However, it is for Cyríon to guide him where he'll use him."

Náidin sighed and took his seat. The Priest's words gave him confidence and a sense of peace.

The Priest continued. "What do your own Dreamings tell you, Lord Gríson?"

"I see his brother leaving our lands and darkness follows; of him, I see nothing. Not even his name. It was the King who received the Dreaming of it."

"Our Dreamings say our sons' names will be known throughout the world." Thalin announced. "So, yes, Kalidin will likely leave as your Dreamings show, Cousin, as will Náidin. What darkness you see in that when we see hope, I cannot fathom."

Lord Gríson glared at the priest. "I will get to the bottom of what poison seeps into our ways and taints even the Dreamings of the Temple. I will seek no more counsel outside those that tend the Body of Cyríon. If the twins are allowed to follow this path, it will destroy our ways."

"That sect is flawed. Those chambers are from where our first Mothers and Fathers were born under Cyríon and his Consort's hands. All the Earthen Folk are part of the Body of Cyríon, as he is our Creator and giver of Dreamings," the Priest replied.

"Is it not better that those that could not live otherwise be put in them and give glory to our Creator?"

"It may have started as a kindness to those unable to live outside their Mother's womb, but tell me, what defect lies in a younger twin that your House consigns them to such a fate?"

"Neither twin is whole as long as they both walk in the world." Lord Gríson looked over at him and Kalidin. "Tell the Priest when you both last had a Dreaming."

"This morning," Náidin answered.

Kalidin shook his head. "I have no Dreamings; I guard my brother while Cyríon communes with him."

The Priest regarded them a moment. "Why do you feel you need to guard him?"

"His Dreamings can last days."

"Would not the support of being part of the Body have been better for the boy?" Lord Gríson gestured to Náidin.

"I see a healthy dwarfling. One that may need his brother's support, but whole in mind and body." The Priest shook his head. "The darkness you fear is in your own heart, Lord Gríson."

"And what if his brother isn't there when these Dreamings last days?"

The Priest arched a brow. "Cyríon, I am certain, would not send such long Dreamings if his Guardian were absent. Don't you see? The boy does not need to enter the Temple, nor the Body as he is already in service to Cyríon. The child is born to the priesthood and follows where he is ordained."

"A compromise then. I will not remove his sash," Lord Gríson looked at all present, "if he is schooled in the Temple as well."

Náidin's senses faded as he began Dreaming.

Words echoed in his mind. "Accept. Be on guard."

The world around him rushed back in. He looked around at the concerned faces, the haze of the Dreaming clearing.

"A waking Dreaming; what says Cyríon, Náidin?" The Priest bowed to him.

"To accept." He then turned to the head of his House. "I will take studies in the Temple as well."

"It is you that will teach us, child." The Priest bowed again before turning to Lord Gríson. "You truly do not see what the boy is? Your traditions blind you. I wonder how many such as Náidin were denied us by your House aligning with the Body."

"And what is it I do not see?"

"An Avatar. One so filled with the spirit of our Creator that he is, in fact, one with Cyríon."

"I am not Cyríon." Náidin scowled.

"Of course, Child." The Priest laughed. "You are his messenger, and in time he will reveal your purpose."

"Do not indulge the child," Gríson sneered.

The priest raised an eyebrow. "I see why his name was not given to you. Had it been you would've withheld it. With the King being the one given it, you were forced to bestow it."

Lord Gríson jabbed his finger into Náidin's chest, "He will bring darkness."

"The darkness is in you, Lord Gríson," the priest admonished.

"I will preserve our ways," Lord Gríson said as he left.

"Kal?"

"Hhhmm?"

Náidin took a deep breath then exhaled in careful measure. "I don't want to be special."

"What makes you think you are?" His brother shoved him.

"The Priest said I'm an Avatar."

"It's just a type of Priest."

Náidin shook his head. "What do I know of guiding the Earthen Folk in Cyríon's teachings?"

Kalidin shrugged. "Don't start doubting your Dreamings now."

Náidin shoved his twin as they trudged up the stair, causing him to stumble forward.

"Wha!! You are definitely not special."

Díja called out to them. "Stop roughhousing on the stair and join the rest of us."

Four groupings of dwarflings stood waiting in the clearing. One of the groups of boys held only ten. The other held twelve, as did one of the girls'. The other group of girls held seven. Náidin grinned at the House Mother. "Sorry, Mistress."

"Join your dorm mates."

Náidin grabbed Kalidin's hand and pulled him to the smaller group. They stood in two columns with gaps. Seeing them lined up so, Náidin let go his brother's hand, with head bowed and shoulders slumped, moved to the empty spot at the back leaving Kalidin to fill in the one in front.

Once in place, Díja addressed the dwarflings. "We welcome Kalidin and Náidin, Sons of Thalin of Nerhaed House. With their addition, the last of the dwarflings born in your year have arrived, and your studies will begin after tomorrow's Day of Introspect. Introduce yourselves now, as tomorrow you are now of age where you will remain silent and fasting after the Feasts of Winter Tide."

The dwarfling next to Náidin smiled at him. "I'm Jer, Son of Malk, of House Feylin."

"Náidin, Son of Th-"

"No need to recite the whole, you've been introduced." Jer chuckled.

"Am I right that the order is our bunks?"

"Aye, I'm third top left."

The dwarfling before him turned. "Welcome, Náidin. We're bunkmates. I'm Lúc, Son of Vryn of House Feylin, Jer's cousin."

Soon the boys had all exchanged their names and those of the other three groups. Díja led them back to the dorms. The chatter ended as they entered. Náidin dropped his gaze to the floor and pursed his lips tight together. He stood waiting his turn to enter his room. He recited the Invocation in his mind when he noticed Jer had begun his turn.

Cyríon clear my mind, so I may think.

Cyríon clear my eyes, so I may see.

Cyríon clear my ears, so I may hear.

Cyríon open my heart, so I may love.

Cyríon guide me, so I am not lost.

Cyríon guard me, so I need not fear.

After the fifth cycle, he walked into the dorm. He resisted looking to his brother's bunk as he entered. Among the soft sounds of the other eleven breathing, he could pick out Kalidin's familiar sound. He paused and let the cycle run in his head again; pulling his thoughts inward before retrieving his nightshirt from his chest.

He bit his lip to keep from gasping at the shock of the cold as he splashed himself from the fall in the bathing room. He greatly preferred a soak in steaming water, to a cold rinse.

Purified, dried, and dressed, he made his way to his bunk and climbed in. He forced down the panic of not being nearer Kalidin and drifted off to sleep, repeating the invocation in his head.

CHAPTER 3:
KALIDIN'S 2ND VERSE

Kalidin climbed out of his bunk, changed to his school robes and then headed for the Sanctuary. He knelt, staring into the still pool. A wee smile turned the corners of his mouth as he thought of the day before, and his brother resisting the Name Day meditation. Or had he? There was something more thought provoking in skipping stones on the cavern lake than kneeling beside a pool.

Try as he might, he could not get his mind to turn inwards. Regardless, he remained kneeling all day. His empty stomach plagued him, as did his thoughts. He worried about his brother. He couldn't say why, he just knew deep inside something was not as it should be.

It occurred to him, that none of the feet he'd seen all day were his brother's. The chime sounded, letting him know he could return to the room for sleep. He rose to his feet and stretched his legs to return the circulation, before hurrying back to the dorm. He made his way to his brother's bunk, and there he could hear the deep breathing that indicated Náidin's Dreamings.

Kalidin felt remiss, having left his brother by himself all day. The Priest had called him Náidin's Guardian. Thinking about it, he knew it to be true. Yet, he had left the room without checking on his brother. Did the Day of Introspect excuse his duty? His unease all day gave him the answer he sought. He should never leave his brother's side when in a Dreaming.

Let Mistress Díja reprimand him for breaking custom. He crawled up into Náidin's bunk with him and pulled his brother close. Lord Gríson said they were not whole as long as both walked in the world. Perhaps that meant they were only whole together.

Calmness settled over him. His thoughts felt right. Náidin's breath settled into a gentler rhythm and his brow unfurrowed. Kalidin let himself drop off to sleep.

CHAPTER 4:
NÁIDIN'S 2ND VERSE

Náidin awoke to Kalidin being scolded by Mistress Díja. He blinked sleep from his eyes and sat up. Kalidin stood, defiant, just below him. "If it is not me in his, it will be him in mine. Moving one of us to another room won't stop us."

"If you don't want one of you sent to live with another Clan, you will both have to stay in your own beds." Her features were downcast. The prospect of separating them by force appeared distasteful to her.

"Other than arriving last, is there any reason one could not be asked to move so we share the same set?" Náidin asked.

Kalidin and Mistress Díja both looked up at him. Díja shook her head. "I know twins can share a bond near equal to a mating bond. All the more reason you boys need to learn some level of separation."

Náidin sighed.

Kalidin shook his head. "Not when he's in a Dreaming. The Priest called me his Guardian at the feast."

She crossed her arms looking at both of them. After a bit, she threw up her hands. "Get dressed, we'll sort this later."

Náidin watched the House Mistress shuffle out of the room. He raised an eyebrow and looked down at his brother. "You were in my bunk?"

"Aye, you were caught in a Dreaming all day."

"I missed the Day of Introspect?" Náidin frowned.

"Since when does missing meditation bother you?" Kalidin called over his shoulder as he went to go dress.

"I meditate! Just not how they want me." Náidin crawled down. He noted that he and Kalidin were alone in the room. Mistress Díja had addressed them in private.

He pulled his scratchy robe over his head and belted it. He then shoved his feet into the slippers, as he could not find his boots. He ran a brush through his hair haphazard enough to remove the tangles, but not tame his wild locks.

Kalidin stood at the door, waiting. "What did your Dreaming show?"

Náidin shook his head as he walked past his brother. "Nothing I can make sense of yet."

A Priest stood at the front of the room. He smiled at the assembled dwarflings. "Welcome. I will be your academic instructor. You may call me Master Láin. You have had your first participation in the Day of Introspect. I would like you all to tell what you learned about yourselves."

Nikta, the oldest girl in their birth year snorted, "That it's hard to keep my mind clear."

The room erupted in whispers of agreement.

"True, it is very difficult to keep our minds void of any thoughts. But what thought entered your mind?"

"That I wished I had a slice of bread, warm from the oven."

"What does bread like that mean to you?"

Náidin watched the expressions play across Nikta's face. "It makes me happy."

"Why?" Láin prodded.

"It reminds me of my grandmother."

The Priest smiled. "Did you have other thoughts?"

She opened her mouth to speak and then shut it. A frown creased her face. "They all had to do with baking."

"And your grandmother?"

"No. She's the one who taught me though."

"Perhaps, you will be a baker as your trade."

The other dwarflings offered their prominent thoughts during the meditation to the Priest. He nudged them in turn with questions that made some sense of what they learned.

Kalidin finally spoke. "My mind wandered to my brother—the fact he isn't very good at sitting still to meditate. I cleared my mind after that, and thought of nothing. Something felt wrong."

Láin raised an eyebrow and asked, "What felt wrong?"

"While I knelt beside the pool, I could not place it. When it was time to go, I knew what was wrong. Náidin was not with us."

Náidin lowered his head. He'd caused his brother stress when he should be learning more about himself.

"Náidin, why were you not with the others?"

He breathed in deep, letting it out slow and measured before answering. "I was caught in a Dreaming."

"What insight did Cyríon give you?"

He furrowed his brow and shook his head. "I do not understand what I saw."

"You will when your visions come to pass." The Priest smiled. "It is true then, an Avatar and his Guardian. You will both walk a difficult path in the future."

Lúc stood.

Láin nodded to him. "Speak."

"What is an Avatar?"

"One born with a greater affinity with our creator. They are priests born to their calling and directed by Cyríon through intense Dreamings. They do not enter the Temple to serve, nor are they subject to the restrictions of other clergy."

Náidin sunk in his seat as the other dwarflings turned to stare in his direction. All their eyes on him caused him to grow hot as blood rushed to his face.

"Treat him as you would any other dwarfling," their instructor admonished. The others murmured as they returned their attention to the Priest.

Master Láin continued, "Now that we have discussed your first Day of Introspect, we will move on to Governance."

Náidin grinned and swung his feet in anticipation.

"The Houses began with the First Fathers. Our writings tell us, each woke on a different day. This order became their ranking. The first to wake was, Nerhaed."

Náidin frowned. How could that be? The king was not a member of their House, nor were the kings of the other three Clans. Lord Gríson would rule if their House were ranked so high. Not wanting to draw more attention, he kept his thoughts to himself.

"At one time, there were no Clans, and the tunnels our people lived in during the Time of Ice were connected. A great earthquake collapsed thoroughfares sundering the Earthen Folk into four communities. These became the four Clans, each ruled by their King. It was not until the last Avatar walked amongst as that we were reunited with our lost kin."

One of the girls stood.

"Palía, you have a question?" Master Láin asked.

"Why are some in a House considered lesser than others?"

"For order, the Eldest member of a House sits on the Council and represents all under them. The next eldest line in the family ranks as second and can sit on behalf of their House should the Elder line be unavailable. All others are equal.

CHAPTER 5:
KALIDIN'S 3RD VERSE

As they readied to return to the dorms, Master Láin approached them. "The edict that Náidin take studies in the Temple does not extend to you, Kalidin." He smiled. "However, I would be loath to separate a Guardian from their Charge. Will you take lessons alongside your brother?"

Would I? Could it help me protect Náidin? "Am I allowed?"

"All are welcome who wish to learn. It is a shame it is forced on your brother."

"I will." Kalidin nodded. "Uhm, are Guardians also a type of Priest?"

"What do you think?"

Kalidin rolled his eyes. "That you don't know."

"Then perhaps you and Náidin can teach us something. The last an Avatar walked amongst our people he opened our Halls to the sky."

"Is an Avatar always a twin?" Náidin asked.

"Yes, in fact, always the second." The Priest squeezed Náidin's shoulder. "We don't understand why, but the first never receives Dreamings, though the Avatar's Dreamings are considered to belong to both."

Kalidin smiled as Náidin turned to him, a scowl on his face. "I am sorry; I do not always share them."

He flicked Náidin on the forehead. "I don't mind when you contemplate them first."

His brother rubbed his forehead and stuck his tongue out.

"Some Dreamings will be meant for you, alone, Náidin." Master Láin beckoned them to follow.

As their class returned to the Dorms, he and Náidin followed the Priest to the Temple. He lead them into a sparse room; just a bench in the middle. The soft glow of the ceiling bathed the room in white light. He knew the dorm had light balls, but to see the whole ceiling illuminated made him catch his breath. Their humble home used oil lamps and candles.

"Your family lives outside the mountain, do they not?"

Kalidin nodded. "Aye."

"First time seeing one of the ancient Light Rooms?"

The twins nodded.

"Sit." The Priest gestured to the bench.

Kalidin placed a hand on the small of Náidin's back and moved him to the bench. As they settled in, Náidin looked up at Master Láin. "What now?"

Láin produced two spheres, one of malachite, and the other azurite. "I believe these stones represent your baby names. Which to whom?"

Kalidin took the malachite orb, and Náidin, the azurite.

"Concentrate on the spheres. Think only of them, see only them, when you have shut all else out, you should be able to hear the music."

"Music?" Náidin asked.

"Cyríon's song. It is said, in our early days, we did not have Dreamings. That we heard music, and those drawn to it became our first priests."

Kalidin furrowed his brow. "Why do we have Dreamings now?"

"Cyríon may guide us, but he does not control us. Many priests withheld his teachings from the others. Sharing only what they saw fit."

"Why are there still priests, then?" Náidin cocked his head.

"To gather and keep the knowledge we are given." He smiled. "I will return shortly."

Kalidin turned on the bench to put his back against his brother's. He held the malachite orb in his hands; the weight of it served as a reminder of his task. He noticed the coolness of the stone warmed to match his hands as he traced the banded lines with his eyes. He felt calmness wash over him as the faint notes of song reached his ears. Or did it?

The music contained an ethereal quality. More than that, he realized the song came from inside him. He could feel it more than hear it as a vibration that started in his belly washing out in waves, making his fingers and toes tingle. A tear slipped down his face. He finally felt a part of his people. He latched onto the strange melody. His mind flooded with images of distant lands.

The visions faded as footfalls drowned out the music. He sighed as he found himself staring at the malachite in his hands. He turned to see the Priest return. "Master Láin, does the song bring Dreamings when it is heard?"

"What did you see, Kalidin?" Láin asked.

"Places with strange peoples and buildings. Lakes that rushed up onto the land and so vast I could not see the far shore. Buildings that floated and moved on the water, tree-like spires rising from them draped with great curtains."

Náidin turned towards him, a huge grin on his face and his eyes twinkling. "My Dreamings yesterday showed the same!"

Láin chuckled. "It would seem a Guardian is capable of Dreamings through hearing Cyríon's song as of old."

"But what does the Dreaming mean?" Kalidin frowned as he tried to make sense of the images. He understood his twin's earlier answer.

"Dreamings of those in the Temple as well as your parents' give the answer. You will travel far from here. I don't know which human or Starborn cities you might have seen. However, the water is likely the seas or oceans, great salty bodies of water. The floating buildings would be ships, and the curtains, sails. You have seen a boat?"

Náidin nodded. "Father took as fishing last summer on the river."

"Ships are much larger boats. The ones in your Dreamings are moved by the winds."

Kalidin considered the Priest and Náidin's words. "Have you traveled, Master Láin?"

"Once, when I was young." Láin nodded. "I was chosen to go out and observe. I traveled with a trade caravan to the seaport of Lysandra."

"Will you teach us about your journey?" Kalidin perked up.

"We can include some in your lessons in the Temple." The Priest smiled. "You may both return to your dorm. Take the orbs, practice finding Cyríon's Song."

"This is it? My-our lesson?" Náidin inquired.

"It is the beginning."

Kalidin crawled into his bunk. He pulled out the malachite orb and placed it on his chest, his hands wrapped around the smooth surface. The low light of sleep time obscured the banded pattern. Still, he traced the patterns best he could. Letting it fill his mind.

He awoke well rested if nothing else. The song and visions had eluded him.

CHAPTER 6:
NÁIDIN'S 3RD VERSE

Náidin found the more he practiced finding Cyríon's Song, the more he noticed an absence of music around him. He leaned forward, eager to learn about it.

"There are two songs common to all Earthen Folk. One is the song mothers sing to their children. This lullaby is the Song of Welcome, and awakens Cyríon's Song in them. Though only members of the Temple hear that music, all Earthen Folk carry it within them. The second is the Song of Mourning and the only one-"

Náidin knit his brow and stood.

"You have a question, Náidin?"

"Why are songs only sung to infants and for the dead?"

"Music is sacred to Cyríon." Master Láin replied. "As I was saying, the Song of Mourning is the only one all Earthen Folk sing."

Náidin scowled at the answer as he plopped back into his seat. Something deep within him didn't accept the answer. An elbow to his ribs brought his wandering mind back to the lecture. He scowled at his twin.

"Whatever is running about that brain of yours, just stop."

He huffed.

"Náidin, Kalidin, would you like to share with the class what is more important than this lecture?" Láin asked.

"I still do not understand why only those two songs. It feels wrong." Náidin blurted.

"You're just upset you got in trouble for making the sounds from Cyríon's Song on the way to breakfast." Kalidin rolled his eyes.

"I see your next lesson in the Temple should be with the Keepers of the Song." Master Láin shook his head.

Náidin grinned.

"Those are the only pieces, common to all Earthen Folk. There are also regional songs for the festivals in the other Kingdoms."

Náidin's smile faded. *The other Kingdoms? But not here?*

Master Láin chuckled. "I see that look on your face, Náidin. If you want to know why there are none in Akekelth, look no further than when your own House ruled."

Lúc rose to his feet.

Master Láin called on him.

"If his House ruled, how does it exist after exile?"

"Nerhaed's primary and secondary lines produced only daughters five generations back. Only the tertiary line still carries the House name."

Náidin knew they were distantly related to King Caidél. Now he understood the connection. Their King was descendent of the eldest daughter those five generations ago. He had to bite his lip to keep from bursting out in laughter. It came out a snort.

Lúc rolled his eyes. "Don't know why you think it's funny."

"What? That you thought my family lost rule by exile?" Náidin raised an eyebrow. "Not what I found funny. Lord Gríson must know we are a third line, and that, knowing him, is funny."

"Nerhaed House's Lord is a Traditionalist," Nikta laughed, "And a third child is against tradition."

"You think he may want a match between you or Kalidin with the

King's eldest granddaughter to regain your House's standing?" Jer asked.

"I would think matching his own son, our cousin Fen, would serve his ego better," Kalidin added, shaking his head.

"You can discuss your lineages and political intrigues in your Governance session. Today is cultural customs," Master Láin brought them back on subject.

"Why did our House forbid other songs?" Kalidin asked.

"Nerhaed House has a strong affinity to Cyríon's Order. Your ancestor felt music should be only in service of our Creator as it was first given to those who served."

Náidin sighed. It still felt wrong to him to withhold music.

Náidin noted Master Láin took them on a different route through the temple. As they passed one corridor, something brushed at the corners of his mind. He felt a shudder crawl up his spine.

Kalidin placed a hand on his shoulder. He turned towards his brother to see his features pinched into a frown. Náidin shook his head. His brother sighed. Náidin knew his brother would only leave it for now.

"We are not working with the healers today?" Náidin asked.

"Given your interest in music, no." Láin replied.

They entered a round chamber. Priests and priestesses sat on the concentric benches, their eyes closed. Cyríon's Song filled the room, but not the same as he heard it within. Some held tubes to their lips as fingers covered and uncovered holes, others plucked at strings or beat skins stretched over round wooden frames with a stick.

Master Láin leaned close to his ear. "They are called instruments." He pointed to each area as he named them, "Flutes, harps, and drums."

Náidin felt compelled to pick up a drum. His hand slid across the skin as a smile grew. He closed his eyes and connected to the song. His first strikes were discordant as he tested the new movement. The others stilled their playing.

Someone pressed against his back and guided his arms to hold the drum and striker properly. He let Cyríon's Song play through him.

"The young Avatar is a Keeper of the Song," spoke an unfamiliar feminine voice behind him. "Though he is not meant for here."

Náidin opened his eyes, his playing faltered. He twisted to look up at the Priestess, with tears welling in his eyes as he held the drum to his chest.

"Keep it young one. It called to you and is yours."

Náidin squirmed as he sat in meditation. Stillness did not come easy to him. He leaned back against Kalidin, the solid presence of his twin calming him. Master Láin would certainly physically separate them next session.

The azurite orb in his hands blurred as Cyríon's song rose from deep inside him. Visions of faraway lands filled his mind, as it had every session for both of them. This time they morphed to the festival field. A woman played an instrument held beneath her chin with a stick. She wasn't of the Earthen Folk. *Go with her.*

The vision faded as he felt pressure against his mind. Náidin reached for the presence. The physical world faded from his senses, or at least as he knew it. The sensation of floating in a viscous fluid replaced the solidness of his brother at his bank, the bench beneath them and the cool air.

He felt neither cold nor warm. He could feel the heavy fluid with each breath. The sensation made his mind scream for an end to the nightmare he stumbled into.

His brother's steady breathing and the ambient noises faded, the only sound around him were the near imperceptible movement of the liquid as it ebbed and flowed through his nose with each breath. The current tickled his lip. Yet, Cyríon's Song still welled up inside him.

Darkness enveloped him as much as the thick fluid that clung to his skin and invaded his airway. Deeper at his core fear and loneliness bubbled up. The feelings belonged to the presence that touched his mind.

Who?

The other clung to his mind tighter at the attempted contact. Náidin tried to recoil. He could not regain his own senses. Other minds, just as empty of words, crowded in.

Another mind, one more ordered, twisted the other minds to its purpose. It asked questions, which the other minds aligned to bring jumbled visions. He felt his own mind being pulled at and balked.

Náidin awoke snuggled against his brother. He frowned, as he didn't remember crawling out of his own bunk. The others chatted as they dressed in their uniforms and some arranged their sashes. Winter Tide. Feasting all day! And today marked their fifteenth annual.

Náidin nudged his brother. "Kal, get up!"

Kalidin groaned and cracked an eye open. "You are far too happy."

"We get to go to the feast, and see mother and father." Náidin rolled out of his brother's bunk.

He dressed and pulled his House sash on. He looked in his trunk at his new drum. He caressed the skin before picking it up.

Kalidin nudged him over as he started to dress. "You should leave it."

Náidin shook his head. "I'm bringing it."

"Please. Leave it," Kalidin pleaded, "Lord Gríson is likely to be in a foul enough mood."

He frowned as he lowered it back into his chest. "I wish he'd leave me alone."

The cold air stung the inside of his nose as he took a deep breath causing him to shiver. The bonfires spread out along the riverbank, and the smells of roasting meat already filled the air. He smacked Kalidin on the back of his head and then took off down the stair to the valley.

A few steps from the bottom, his feet slipped from beneath him, and he slid down the last few steps on his rear. He lay at the base of the stairs and looked up at his laughing twin. "Not funny."

"Since you're in one piece, it is." Kalidin held out a hand.

Náidin took it and let his brother pull him to his feet. "Still not funny."

"Sure, it is." Kalidin gave him a shove. "You're an idiot."

He huffed as he stomped off towards their House's tables. The soft heavy flakes that fell around him dispelled his annoyance and filled him with joy. So much so, he started humming. Not Cyríon's Song this time, just something that came to him.

"Oi!" He turned to glare at Kalidin, who had just smacked him on the back of the head.

"You can't be doing that."

"I want to go to a Winter Tide Festival where I can," Náidin grumbled.

They rounded a corner a few feet later to come face to face with Lord Gríson and his son, Fen. "The Priests tell me you do well in your studies, Náidin. That you have a calling as a Keeper and do well assisting the healers."

"The Keepers say I am one, but not meant to join them, Milord."

"Then perhaps you would consider joining the healers."

"It is not my path."

"I want you introduced to the Body after tomorrow."

Náidin glanced at Kalidin, a frown on his face. "Only Priests are allowed near."

"The head of the order has agreed that your studies have shown you to be a Priest and is granting you time to learn their ways.

"Just me?"

"Ah, yes," Lord Gríson smiled. "Kalidin, walk with me, and Fen. Náidin, join your parents."

CHAPTER 7
KALIDIN'S 4TH VERSE

Kalidin followed behind Lord Gríson and Fen. His steps becoming more hesitant the further down the river they moved. "Milord, where are we going?"

"I've arranged for you to foster in another Kingdom until the Blossom Festival."

He stopped. "Milord, I am Náidin's Guardian."

"So Láin and the heads of the other orders claim." Lord Gríson turned towards him. "You will accompany Fen on his negotiations with Prinkelth. I think the distance will allow your brother to honor our traditions. That and there is a lass I want you to acquaint yourself with in hopes a bonding might grow in the future."

"You could've at least let me say goodbye to him."

Fen placed a hand on Kalidin's shoulder. "I'm sure your brother will be fine."

"I did not want a fuss." Lord Gríson raised an eyebrow. He then turned to his son. "Keep a hand on him, and once you make it to the wagon, blindfold him and bind his hands until you make camp."

"Is our young cousin a prisoner, father?"

"Nay. He has far too close a bond with his twin. It is best he not know the way home, or he is likely to be a fool and attempt to return on his own."

Kalidin watched Lord Gríson return up the path, disdain for the head of their House welling up inside. He looked over at Fen. "Well, cousin?"

"Father only wishes what is best for all, Kalidin."

Kalidin snorted. "Lord Gríson only wishes for my brother to be where he wants him and our House to serve his whims."

"He is the head of our House." Fen gripped his arm and pulled him further down the path.

"You agree with him?" Kalidin asked. He had to jog to keep from falling onto his face at the pace Fen set.

"I obey him." Fen shrugged.

"Why during Winter Tide? Will we still meditate tomorrow?"

"No, we will not." Fen shook his head and then sighed. "Even he can't enter the Halls of Learning to remove you."

CHAPTER 8:
NÁIDIN'S 4TH VERSE

N áidin sat picking at his food. His eyes scanned the paths to their table every few seconds. *Where is Kal?*

He sighed in relief as Lord Gríson came into view. Then coldness washed over him as he noticed Kal did not accompany him. Náidin began to shake, his breaths coming in gasps.

His mother and father surrounded him, though he could not focus on what they said.

His mother rounded on Lord Gríson. "Where is my other son?" She bellowed. The mention of his brother caught his attention.

"He'll return next festival." Lord Gríson smiled.

Náidin curled in on himself sobbing.

"Where did you send Kalidin?" Master Láin asked as he approached.

"Prinkelth." Lord Gríson answered. "I plan on grooming the boy as a liaison and a possible match for their Princess."

"You interrupted his time of learning for this?" Thalin growled.

"Come, you tell me you haven't all had Dreamings he won't finish his Ten Year?" Lord Gríson smirked.

"You evidently are still blind to Náidin in your Dreamings, Milord."

Master Láin answered. "Kalidin is not meant to leave here, alone."

His mother smoothed his hair as she rocked him. "Hush; we will bring your brother back."

Master Láin called over two Acolytes. "Go with Thalin. Retrieve Kalidin on orders of the Temple."

"Ah, by what authority Láin?" Lord Gríson narrowed his eyes. "The boy is of my House, and answers to me."

"Both take lessons in the Temple though their path is not to serve there. They are both Acolytes, as Avatar and Guardian, and members of the Temple. They are, as you wished Náidin to be, both in service to Cyríon."

Náidin woke as a warm hand ruffled his hair.

"I thought you were excited about the Festival? And here I return to find you sleeping."

"You left me," Náidin whispered as he turned towards his brother.

"Not by choice." Kalidin pulled him up into a hug.

He clung to his brother, afraid he'd disappear again.

Kalidin gave him a playful cuff on the ear. "I'm starving. Let's get some roast."

"Just some gylfë to drink."

Kalidin sighed and nodded. "I'll be right back."

Náidin held tighter to his brother and shook his head.

"Promise."

Náidin took a deep breath and let go his twin. "Sorry," he mumbled. He watched Kalidin walk to the cook fires.

He could hear Master Láin arguing with Lord Gríson. "How many times must the priests and the child tell you Cyríon forbids service where you will him to be?"

"What harm in having him tend the Body?"

"He is not an initiate of that Sect." Láin argued. "What were you thinking, separating a bonded pair in such a manner?"

"I gained the head of the Sect's approval to have him initiated. What I am doing is trying to give them some semblance of separate lives." Lord Gríson spat. "Had his heretic of a mother allowed the breaking of their bond when they were born and relinquished the younger as our House tradition demands, we would not be having these difficulties."

"How is it my wife is a heretic when she goes against only our House's traditions, yet you ignore both our People's and House's traditions when it suits your agenda?" Thalin stood toe to toe with his cousin.

"I should sanction your whole family."

"Do it then." Thalin held his head high. "I will petition the King to commission a new House from my line."

"I will not give you that satisfaction. I will not treat with you as an equal on the Council." Lord Gríson stalked off.

Náidin wiped tears from his eyes as he took a seat at the table. "I am sorry to cause such trouble."

"It is not you that causes trouble." His father squeezed his shoulder.

Kalidin slid onto the bench beside him. One hand holding two mugs, and the other with a plate piled with meat and vegetables.

Náidin took one of the mugs from his brother, the warmth soaking into his hands. He took a deep breath of the steaming golden liquid. He loved the smell of the juniper and birch infused in honey.

He sipped at the thick liquid as he eyed Kalidin's plate. His appetite returning, he snagged a sliver of roasted meat.

Kalidin chuckled as he lifted his plate and slid half the food onto the one hidden below. "Knew you'd want some."

Náidin grinned at his brother as he took the fork his twin held up as he pushed the plate in front of him.

Náidin and Kalidin followed Master Láin past the other students and to the Temple for the Day of Introspect. Instead of the Light Room, he led them to a deep cavern with a pool of water. They knelt beside the water.

Náidin felt the other minds crowd his again. As before, he felt transported from the world around him into a visceral fluid. Fear, pain, and loneliness filled him. He knew the feelings did not belong to him.

He endured their touch as he knelt trying to look within himself. The woman and her strange instrument surfaced again in his thoughts; the vision much stronger and clearer than before. He saw himself sitting by a fire in the woods with a copy of the same instrument beneath his chin. Kalidin sat near him with another. A man busied himself with roasting birds over the fire.

Náidin put away his quill and ink stone. He stretched his hands to relieve the tension from writing practice. He turned to his brother. "To keep peace in our family, I will go see the Body today. Will you still go to the Temple?"

Kalidin nodded. "Aye. The Healers will likely need my assistance today."

Náidin's shoulders slumped. "Do you think Néda's child will be born today?"

"Her labor began late last night, from what I heard Master Láin discussing." He nodded.

"Perhaps, Lord Gríson's wishes can wait a day." Náidin frowned. "I did not give my word to honor his arrangement."

"Attend the birth first then. I can help in the Apothecary after, while you seek the Body and appease the old curmudgeon."

Náidin raised an eyebrow. "You have not been paying close enough attention to our lectures on birthing if you think that is possible."

"And neither have you if you don't realize it is."

Náidin smirked at his twin. "I concede, though I fear it is not probable."

Náidin knew Néda agreed to him and his brother assisting the birth. What he hadn't known was that the Healers would verbally guide him in assisting the delivery. Yet here he sat on a stool between the new mother's knees as she sat in the birthing chair, a wet and squalling newborn in his hands.

The attending Midwife placed a hand on his shoulder. "Hand the babe to her mother."

Náidin nodded and did as instructed. Néda smiled as she took her daughter. Kalidin prepped the infants cord as directed and cut it.

"A blessing on your hearth, Néda." Náidin grinned. "What will you call her?"

"Amethyst."

The Midwife cleared her throat.

Náidin looked over. "You are both dismissed. You did well."

"Thank you Mistress."

"We still have three bells before we must return to the dorm." Kalidin stated as he began scrubbing his hands.

"A shorter time is likely best." Náidin sighed.

Kalidin chuckled. "He did say he wanted you introduced. Surely that is enough time for that."

"You do not have to go." Master Láin stood before the passage that had caused him to shudder when he'd gone to the Keepers of the Song.

"I know."

Láin moved aside letting him pass down the hall. Náidin took a deep breath and started down the passage. Each step became more difficult to take. His body was tense, and his thoughts grew jumbled.

At last, he stood in the doorway. He saw a priest in meditation amidst large metal boxes with frosted glass lids. He felt the other presences invade his thoughts again. Their fear and pain pervasive, but tinged with a sense of hope.

He could hear the priest's low monotone words both audibly and as a pull on his thoughts.

He spun and ran from the room seeking the comforting presence of Kalidin. The pressure of all the other minds in his head consumed his conscious thought. His awareness of his surroundings more instinctive as he sought his twin.

Distance from the room allowed him to order his own thoughts and to push against the mind controlling the collective.

Náidin separated each mind in his own and then stilled them one by one. He could feel the fear and pain leave as each one quieted. The controlling one became panicked. The other minds no longer clinging to his, he shoved the last one away.

His senses returned to him; his body left shaking. He could hear people running in the corridors. Alarms started ringing.

Master Láin appeared in the door. "Kalidin, get your brother out of the Temple. Now!"

CHAPTER 9:
KALIDIN'S 5TH VERSE

"Kalidin, a word with you." Mistress Díja intercepted them as they walked into the dorm hall. "Náidin go put the drum away and clean up for dinner."

Náidin glanced at him, eyebrows raised.

Kalidin nodded. "Go."

He watched his brother shuffle off to their room and then turned to the House Mother. "Your office?"

She nodded and led him to her door. Once in she sat down at her desk. Kalidin felt her gaze on him as he took his time settling into the chair across from her.

Díja cleared her throat. "I know the Priests say you are a Guardian; however, I'm worried at the depth of your bond with your brother."

"Is it truly a problem?" He sighed in relief that it wasn't about the commotion in the Temple. He still wasn't sure what he'd witnessed his brother do through their connection.

"I've discussed it with the Temple, and they've agreed the bond needs to be broken." She smiled.

He supposed the smile was to ease what fear he had. "Is it not normal for an Avatar and Guardian to bond?"

"It is. However, the fact he panics when you're separated is a sign the bond is too deep."

"Why talk with only me?"

"It is at your end, the bond will be severed."

Kalidin felt a chill prickle his skin. "When?"

"Tonight, when all are sleeping." She came around the desk and wrapped her arms around his shoulders. "It has to be now before it deepens further."

"Why now? Is it truly so wrong?" He felt an edge of panic at the thought. If it disturbed him, how would Náidin act when he found out?

She held his head against her and smoothed his hair. "It isn't wrong. However, it can become dangerous for both of you. Especially your brother."

"We aren't telling him, are we?" Tears slipped down his cheeks.

"No, we are not." She sighed. "It is better he not know, for he needs to reach back out to you reflexively. If he knew it was severed, he might consciously hold back."

"I don't understand, Mistress Díja." He felt a lump in his throat.

"A Guardian needs his bond to the Avatar to protect him. It should not be so deep the Avatar can't function properly without his Guardian around."

Kalidin sighed. "Why are you telling me, and not Master Láin?"

"Given Lord Gríson's desire for Náidin to enter the Temple, what do you suppose you'd have done if he spoke with you?" She pushed back and held him by the shoulders.

He looked down at his lap. "I would've taken him and run."

"No one wants to see both of you choose exile. Not even Lord Gríson in his own twisted way." She waved her hand to dispel ill luck. "I've been watching you both these five years. As it is my duty to care for the children under my watch."

"What if the bond gets too deep again?"

44

"Reconnected bonds are never so deep. The deepest it should redevelop, given you're twins, is close to a matrimonial bond. As your current bond stands, it is already deeper than one."

"Meaning neither of us could take a wife later?"

Díja nodded. "As rare as identical twins are we know many are celibate due to their bond. What you both are is rarer still. Not all are Avatar and Guardian."

"That isn't what worries you then, is it?"

"No, it isn't. What worries me is the death of one of you would be the death of both if it deepens further."

She placed a piece of candy on the desk. "Make sure Náidin eats that before bed, it will keep him asleep."

Kalidin picked it up and looked at it. "So you want me to betray his trust?"

She sighed and nodded, her eyes downcast.

"Do you at least have one that looks different for me?"

She placed a second candy on the desk. "To protect him, you may find you have to do things he will not approve of on occasion."

"Do you know what you are asking of me?" Kalidin's hand shook as he pocked both candies. "I started studying Guardians in the Temple records. I am of the Earthen Folk, but not one with them. I am one only with my brother."

"You fear having no place." She pulled him into a hug again.

"I've tried to connect to Cyríon's Song on my own outside the Temple; I fail every time." He looked up. "Promise it won't be permanent."

"Náidin, what happened earlier?" Kalidin placed an arm around his brother's shoulder.

"I don't know." He shook his head. "I just know that what I felt was wrong and I made it right."

"We should talk with Master Láin about it in the morning." He pulled out the candies. He popped one into his mouth and nudged his brother to take the other.

"Where did you get these?" Náidin smiled.

"Mistress Díja gave them to me when she spoke with me."

"She must be pleased with you," Náidin sighed, "I was afraid that maybe I'd caused you to break some rule again."

"We've come to an understanding of my duty to you." Kalidin smacked his brother on the shoulder. "Now in bed with you."

They settled into their bunks, and Kalidin listened for the signs his brother had dropped off to sleep. He, himself could not. He heard the other dwarflings' various snores as all the others found sleep.

He heard the door open. Kalidin sat up to see Mistress Díja lead Master Láin in. They beckoned him to follow.

Kalidin slid out of bed, and then with a last glance at his brother, he followed Master Láin out as Mistress Díja settled on the edge of his bunk.

As the door closed, Kalidin sighed. "I don't like this."

"Understood."

He followed Master Láin to the Healers Halls. He caught the hushed worried tones regarding a body being gone. All talk stopped as they noticed he was there.

"Lay here." Master Láin patted a bed.

Kalidin settled on the mattress. He took a shuddering breath.

"I want you to concentrate only on my voice," the Priest continued.

He closed his eyes and waited. Master Láin began to sing. Kalidin let all other sounds disappear. As the song circled back around the fourth time, he felt emptiness inside. His eyes flew open as he began shaking with quiet sobs.

The Priest stopped his chanting and pulled him into an embrace. "Hush."

"With the loss of the Order of Cyríon's Body, was it wise to break a bond between Guardian and Avatar?" A healer asked.

"His brother should reach for him again."

Kalidin felt Láin gather him up as he cried into the Priest's shoulder.

"Could it have not waited?" The healer persisted. "We know not what forces attacked us."

"My Dreamings tell me the boys will leave us soon."

"You don't think they betrayed Cyríon? Why bother if they are to be exiled?" the healer inquired.

Kalidin tried to push away from Láin.

"Are you blind to Cyríon's will?" Láin countered as he held Kalidin tighter.

"Surely Cyríon would not so cruelly destroy those in the chambers?"

"My brother is right. He corrected a wrong." Kalidin scowled at the other Priest. "He freed them from pain and fear."

"You did not owe him an answer, child." Láin chided.

"An Avatar's action would uphold Cyríon's will, not hinder it," the healer asserted.

"Exactly." Láin replied as he pushed past the other Priest. "Think on that."

"Will we be sent away?" Kalidin asked as Láin carried him back to the dorm.

"Not in exile. How or why you will leave is not given to me. Just that you will leave."

How could they leave? Kalidin knew if he needed to protect his brother, he would. Who would take in two dwarflings?

Mistress Díja and Master Láin assisted him to climb in beside Náidin on his upper bunk. He pulled his brother close to him. A smile spread across his face as he felt his twin caress his mind.

Kal?

I am here. He sighed and dropped into sleep.

CHAPTER 10:
NÁIDIN'S 5TH VERSE

Náidin woke to Kalidin's elbow in his ribs. He shifted to give his brother more room. His sleep held no Dreamings, so why was Kalidin in his bed rather than his own?

He gave Kal's shoulder a shake. His twin grumbled and burrowed further into the blankets.

Náidin huffed. It was not like Kal to be hard to wake. He placed his hand on his brother's forehead. *No sign of fever.*

Something felt off. More than waking next to his twin when a Dreaming hadn't been given to him and oblivious to the others having left the room. More than Kal not waking easily.

He closed his eyes and turned his mind inward. Cyríon's Song ebbed and rose as it flowed through him. Why was the song prominent? He frowned as he searched for the ever-present bond with his brother. His chest constricted, causing his breath to catch as what should be there eluded him.

"Cyríon, guide me." He whispered.

The song quieted. And there, muted, he felt his brother. He latched on to the presence in his mind, his breaths coming easier as the edge of panic evaporated.

He mentally poked at the haze between them. Kal elbowed him, breaking his concentration.

Náidin opened his eyes to find, his twin staring at him, one eyebrow raised.

He felt his face warm. Never had he tried to push into his brother's thoughts before. "I'm sorry." He frowned. "It feels… different."

Kal reached over and thumped Náidin on his forehead. "It's supposed to. Promise you won't do that again."

"It was wrong." He sighed. "Promise."

Kalidin nodded. "I'm sorry, too."

"For?"

"I'm happy it worked as they'd hoped. I let Master Láin sever our bond to protect you."

"Kal? Are you well?"

Kalidin chuckled. "Aye. The only thing Lord Gríson seems to have been right about is our bond was too strong."

"We're still bonded." He gave his twin an incredulous look.

"Thank Cyríon. The short time it was gone…" Kalidin shivered.

Náidin propped himself up on an elbow. "If it were gone, how is it there?"

"You reached for me."

Náidin scowled. "What does it all mean?"

"If Mistress Díja is correct, that we can be more independent." Kalidin gave him a nudge. "Or rather you can. Seems Guardians have more independence in a deep bond than Avatars."

Náidin sat up and stretched. His thoughts crowded his mind. What if Kalidin left to join Fen now? Could he endure it? Could he have if he had known his twin would leave before? As he felt his chest constrict again, he took deep breaths and sought solace in the song within.

"Shall we test it?" He turned to Kal.

"Hhhmm." Kalidin blinked at him as he roused from nodding off.

"Test? Ah, the bond."

Náidin nodded.

"How?"

"Join Fen in Prinkelth."

"That's a little extreme. And what if you need me during a Dreaming?" Kalidin rolled onto his side.

"I'll trust in Master Láin and Mistress Díja to keep watch."

"I fear for what may be after what you did yesterday." He shook his head.

"Trust my Dreamings. I am in no danger."

"And if you can't bare the distance between us?"

"I'll be miserable until you return for the Blossom Festival."

Kalidin sat up and pulled Náidin into a hug. "No."

Master Láin rushed Náidin down the passage to the Keepers of the Song. He found himself having to jog to keep up. He glanced over his shoulder at his brother, who stood near the hall that lead to the Healers' Halls. He felt his breath catch.

He's not even out of sight. How do you plan to last the week? He filled his lungs, letting his belly expand, and then let it out measured. It helped ease the edge of panic.

Master Láin stopped before the chamber and turned. He placed a hand on Náidin's shoulder. "Are you well?"

"Aye. Just off balance."

The priest smiled. "Don't push Kalidin away."

Náidin smirked. "Is it even possible?"

"It is tenuous at the moment. It will solidify if you leave it be."

"Staying apart won't sever it again, will it?" Náidin scowled.

"Only if you wish it." Master Láin nodded. "You will train to not seek the bond."

"To give my brother his privacy." He nodded.

Master Láin squeezed Náidin's shoulder and smiled.

Taking a deep breath, he opened himself to Cyríon's Song and entered the chamber. He caressed the drumhead, before pulling the tipper from his belt. He moved it in time to the music, not yet striking the drum, as he got a feel for its weight. He found his place in the circle and joined the music.

CHAPTER 11:
KALIDIN'S 6TH VERSE

Kalidin stood, organizing the tools and supplies needed for sutures. The sniffling dwarfling lass sat huddled in her mother's arms, a dressing wrapped about her hand.

He looked about for one of the Healers. The Head Master nodded to him and pointed from him to the child.

His eyes widened as he pointed to himself.

The priest smiled and turned from him.

Kalidin let out a sigh and moved the wheeled tray to the bedside. He took the dropper from the tincture bottle. "This will make her drowsy and ease her pain," he explained as he administered it to the child.

The girl scrunched her face as she involuntarily swallowed. The child's mother eyed him. "I would rather at least an experienced Acolyte attend."

"The Head Master has appointed me the task."

"Surely you are still in your Ten Year."

"Aye, and for the five years of it, I have been taking lessons in the Temple and am an experienced Acolyte." He didn't add this was the first he did not simply assist.

Kalidin watched as the dwarfling's eyes grew heavy. He then unwrapped the dressing. Assessing the damage, he suppressed the urge to hiss. Keeping his expression neutral, he asked, "What did she cut it on?"

"Her father's hunting knife."

Kalidin rewrapped the hand. "Excuse me. I shall return."

The mother nodded.

He made his way to where the Head Master stood overseeing another acolyte tending a burn.

The priest turned to him. "Is there a problem, Kalidin?"

"Master," he nodded, "the cut is deep; it requires far more than closing the wound."

"Your assessment counters Mistress Síné's." He raised an eyebrow.

"With respect, Head Master, her vision has been failing." Kalidin wiped his palms against his apron.

"And the basis of this assessment?"

"She squints more frequently and has begun putting her nose practically in her work." Kalidin looked the elder priest in the eyes.

"A fair observance and you have passed one, possibly two, of the three tests."

"I was not aware I was to be tested, Head Master."

He chuckled. "Of course not." He placed a hand on Kalidin's shoulder. "Let's have a look at your charge. Shall we?"

Kalidin nodded and led the elder dwarf to the child's bed. The Head Master checked the wound. "Your assessment is correct."

"I will ready the surgery." Kalidin bowed his head to the Head Master.

"I will see to that, you prep the lass."

Kalidin's eyes widened. "Aye."

As the Head Master moved off, the child's mother queried, "Is it truly that damaged?"

"She could lose use of the hand if the damage is not repaired," Kalidin replied, after gauging the dwarfling's alertness. "I shall return with a stronger sedative."

Kalidin dropped into the hot soaking pool in the temple. *What made me think, spending the week in the Temple would be preferable to attending classes? Then again, what would I have chosen?* All the dwarflings of his year were exploring trades the next two moon cycles.

He closed his eyes and contemplated his day in the Healing Halls. His left hand felt cramped after suturing the inner workings of the lass' palm. The Head Master praised his work on all levels. He'd passed all three tests.

The tasks set him served him well in not fretting about Náidin. *Hope his day proved as distracting.*

The water sloshed a bit. He opened eyes to find Master Láin slipping into the pool. The priest smiled. "I heard you did well today."

"Aye." Kalidin stretched. "So they tell me."

"The skill will serve you well soon enough." Láin nodded.

"Will we be exiled after all?" He knit his brow.

"No."

Kalidin sighed in relief.

"When we finish here, I will show you to your bed, and then I must see to your brother."

Kalidin looked about the small room. A narrow cot with a thick mattress and blanket butted up against the wall in line with the door. Next to it, sat a small desk and stool.

The desk held a small glow lamp, inkpot & glass pen, and a covered tray. He surmised the drawer held paper for his reports. The first of which he needed to see to before he crawled into bed.

Next to the door stood a tall wardrobe measuring barely wider than his shoulders. Enough room for a few priests' robes, a nightshirt and a cloak to hang, and a couple pairs of shoes on the floor.

A space designed for function rather than comfort; an acolyte's cell. He grimaced. "Feels more like a closet," he grumbled to himself.

He lifted the lid to find a bowl of mushroom and root stew and a small round of brown bread. There would be no meat while he dwelled with the Healers. Kalidin tucked in to the stew, sopping up the juices with hunks of torn bread. Like the room, just enough to be serviceable.

Kalidin placed the tray outside his door. He returned to the desk to write up his day's observations. He found a thick cloth-bound journal, rather than sheets of paper.

He opened the cover to find a folded piece of paper tucked inside. Kalidin took out the note.

Kalidin,

I have provided both you and Náidin, each, with a journal. May it serve you well in your remaining time at home and on your impending journey.

Master Láin

He dipped the glass nib into the ink and began writing the day's events. Kalidin found writing down the surgery he performed on the dwarfling's hand pulled out information he hadn't realized he'd learned. He gave careful thought to the details as he committed them to paper.

CHAPTER 12:
NÁIDIN'S 6TH VERSE

Náidin paused at the opening of the passage that led to where the Body had been housed. His week with the Keepers neared its end. He not only learned to let Cyríon's Song play through him, but to play and sing the Song of Welcome and the Song of Mourning as well.

His vision blurred as tears welled up. He knew what he did ended the lives of those entombed in the ancient capsules that gave life to the First Fathers and Mothers. *Cyríon, why did you give that task to me? Why did you allow it until now?*

You chose to heed my wishes. Those who kept them did so of their own will. I guide those who follow. The choice is yours to embrace or reject what I show you. Even for one born an Avatar.

Náidin shook his head to clear the fog of the waking Dreaming. Cyríon's response surprised him. Or rather the fact he responded. "Then, I make this choice."

He turned down the passage coming to the room he fled from not so long ago. The capsules, once alight and whirring, stood silent and dark. The dead had no family to contact as those given were struck from the records.

The capsules that sustained them, now their tombs. He wandered through the dim lit room, touching each as he passed. One alcove stood devoid of a capsule.

Náidin paused at the space.

Someday, the why will be revealed to you.

He moved to the middle of the room and positioned his drum. He beat out the tempo of the Song of Mourning. He then raised his voice in song. He sang for each in turn—his voice a harsh whisper and his hands and shoulder blades cramping as he finished 123 rounds.

Náidin strode to the one remaining functional capsule. The one Lord Gríson wanted him in. He closed the lid and pressed his palm against the pad. The door clicked locked, and the light winked out. No one would ever be housed in that one again.

He turned to find a priest in the doorway.

"You sang for the Nameless."

"Were they not still of the Earthen Folk?"

"Why would the one who murdered them care?" The priest sneered.

"I released them from pain and fear." Náidin bowed his head. "I did what I felt called to do. Should I have questioned Cyríon on what that would do?"

"Had you, what decision would you have made?"

He reached out towards the priest with his mind. The presence was familiar, the one who controlled the Body's Dreaming. He used that tentative link they shared that day to send the memory of what he felt. "Now, you tell me what decision you would've made?"

The priest cried out. "That is why?"

Náidin nodded.

"I could bring them together and direct them. See the images their collective minds would muster." He fell to his knees. "I did not feel their fear or pain."

"Do other Earthen Folk Temples have a Body of Cyríon?"

"No, Avatar." The priest looked up. "This is where all began."

Náidin sighed in relief.

"Had I known what they felt," the priest clasped Náidin's hand, "I would've done the same."

"Find a new calling in his service." Náidin smiled and pulled his hand free. He left the priest on his knees and made his way to his cell in the Temple.

He stowed his drum beside his desk, then headed to the bathes. He needed a good long soak. Blessedly the room was empty when he arrived.

He washed up and then slid into the water. He pushed off from the side and floated in the steaming pool on his back. Náidin let his mind wander. What had he learned in the five years of his Ten Year? The basics came first—both in and out of the Temple.

The last year found him and Kalidin acting as Healer Acolytes in the Temple. It suited Kal more, though Náidin took pride in the skills as well. If his Dreamings didn't forbid him to join the Temple, he would seek a position with the Keepers of the Song or the Healers.

The beginning of this fifth year found the dwarflings of his Ten Year, exploring the trades. Perhaps he and Kal would get a chance outside the Temple the next cycle.

He stood up in the pool and looked towards the door to see Kalidin turning away. "The pool will hold us both."

Kal turned towards him. "A week separation."

"What's a couple of days and a chance meeting?" Náidin grinned.

"Incorrigible." Kalidin quipped at his brother as he went to clean up first.

Náidin laughed. The short exchange aside, he realized his time was up. He rose from the pool as Kal scrubbed up under the fall. "I'll see you in two days."

Now Kalidin laughed.

Náidin crawled into his cot, his leather-bound journal in hand. He read over his entries. The first four a brief sentence and the last a detailed account of his honoring the Nameless.

His first four days were more him learning to let go. The lack of fretting where Kal was proved he had achieved what he set out to do. *If mother had not feared what Lord Gríson wanted, would she have let this happen?*

There was comfort in his bond with his brother. However, with the new he felt a freedom he never had with the old bond. One he never knew he wanted.

Náidin rolled out of his cot and sat down at his desk. He needed to write down his thoughts and feelings of these last five days. He felt a bit chagrined he'd avoided exploring them until the chance encounter.

Avoiding his feelings was not the best way to learn to live with his new relationship with his twin. Admittedly, the first two nights, he contemplated searching for his brother's room. Much as he'd done when his parents tried to put them in separate rooms when they were younger.

Náidin read over his reflections once he finished. He then focused inward seeking the bond. It took longer to find it than the last time. This time he didn't probe deeper. Satisfied that it remained in place, he let his surroundings ground him.

CHAPTER 13:
KALIDIN'S 7TH VERSE

K alidin pushed a cart with tinctures, pastilles, and various types of rubs and wrappings through the ward. He stopped at each occupied bed, reading the notes left by the other healers.

His last stop; the lass whose hand he repaired. "Good day, Garnet."

She looked up from her puzzle and grinned. "Master Kalidin!"

Kal laughed. "I am no Master. It is Novice."

"Novice?" She scrunched her face up.

"Aye. It means I still am learning." He sat on the stool beside her bed.

"Oh." She held her bandaged hand out.

Kalidin unwound the bandage and probed the incision. "It has knit well."

"I'm not a shirt."

Kalidin chuckled as he clipped the ends of the stitches. "Of course not. It means the wound has healed."

Garnet hissed as he worked on her hand. He stopped his ministrations and dropped a tincture into a cup. "Here, drink this."

She made a face as she gulped it down. "Blech!"

"It will ease the pain." He rubbed a liniment into the girl's palm.

"It tingles."

"Your hand or the liniment?"

"Where it is."

"Did it tingle before?"

She shook her head.

"Good." He placed a bladder filled with sand in her hand. "Squeeze this."

Garnet closed her fingers around it. Kalidin nodded as he saw all the fingers grip the ball. "Now open your hand flat."

She uncurled her hand, the two middle fingers still a bit crooked.

He placed a board on her lap. "I want you to practice pushing your hand flat on this. On the chime, squeeze the ball to the count of ten."

"Can I use it for my puzzles now?"

Kalidin shook his head. "Continue your exercises with your left until we are sure the other has regained strength."

"Well done, Kalidin." Master Láin placed a hand on his shoulder.

"Thank you, Master." Kalidin turned from his charge. "My time is done?"

"Are your tasks done for the day?"

"Aye."

"Awwwww!" Garnet exclaimed.

Kalidin grinned at the girl. "Soon, you will return home."

"I wish you were not a priest." She pouted.

"I learn with them, but it is not my path." He raised an eyebrow.

"You can be a healer and not a priest?"

"Why do you ask?"

"My Name Day is in two years."

Master Láin chuckled. "The lass has her eye on you for the future, Kalidin."

He looked between the girl and the priest.

"Novice Kalidin is Guardian to an Avatar. His duty lies with his twin."

"He cannot marry?" Garnet pouted.

"It is not forbidden to an Avatar or his Guardian; however, my Dreamings say his Bride dwells where the bells sound on the water."

Garnet pouted.

"There will be another who catches your eye, and a lucky lad he will be." Kalidin ruffled her hair.

Kalidin followed Láin out of the Healer's Halls after stowing the cart.

"Did you truly have Dreamings of my Bride?" His stomach felt unsettled. "There are no Earthen Folk near the Seas. True?"

"True, and yes."

"Did you have to tell the lass?"

"She will forget it soon enough."

"Have you told Náidin?"

"No. There is much about you he will not Dream, and much you need to know that he does not."

Kalidin stopped walking. "You intend to send me on another training."

"What you need is not an honorable path."

"Do I not rejoin my brother?"

"You may seek him when not in your studies."

Kalidin sighed as he fought the numbness spreading inside.

Master Láin pulled him into a hug. "It is not an easy path the both of you have been given."

Kalidin returned to his cell. Would he continue to occupy this room during his new lessons? He found comfort in his simple room. Though he missed a good bit of meat in his meals.

He tucked into the spiced beans and greens on his plate as he thought through Láin's words. One thing he had not done during his separation despite being in the Temple was seek his Dreamings via Cyríon's Song.

Could he connect to it in the Temple with his brother absent? He pushed his plate away and then rummaged through his drawer for his malachite orb. The weight of it in his hand dissipated the unease deep inside him.

He made his way to the Light Room and lowered himself to the bench in the middle. He cupped the orb in his hand, took a deep breath and let go of his thoughts.

The hum of Cyríon's Song vibrated through him, and images filled his mind. A tall lithe girl smiled down at him. His heart fluttered in his chest, despite not seeing her features clearly.

You will know her when you see her. She will bring you happiness in the darkness you walk. Forgive me child, what you must endure.

I will leave both of them grieving me.

It is one branch.

They prepare Náidin to live without me. Do not tell me it is not so.

A perceptive Guardian. If I tell you your fate is writ if you follow your calling will you still?

Until I take my last breath, I will not abandon my brother. Can you find no other way?

If those before you had listened closer this path would not be needed.

Kalidin broke the contact with their creator. "I would rather await young Garnet gaining her name and coming of age," he addressed the empty room. "I will follow the path laid out for me."

He returned his orb to his room and sought the baths.

CHAPTER 14:
NÁIDIN'S 7TH VERSE

Náidin floated in the warm water, his eyes closed. He felt two hands on his shoulder a second before his head dipped beneath the water. He surfaced spluttering and coughing.

"A reminder of why you shouldn't doze in the water." Kalidin stood in the waist deep soaking pool, his arms crossed.

Náidin stuck his tongue out. "I wasn't dozing, just meditating."

"One day, we will leave home. Never lose sense of your surroundings."

He splashed his brother. "Good to see you too."

"It is." Kal sighed. "I will be sent elsewhere for additional training in preparation."

"Away?"

Kalidin shook his head. "Master Láin said I could seek you on my off time, so without you but not away."

"Perhaps I can study beside you?"

Kalidin pulled him into a hug. "No, and do not ask what I must learn."

Náidin sighed.

"Why don't you go study with Father." Kalidin held him out at arm's length and looked him in the eyes. "It will give us an excuse to spend time with them."

"Aye." He lowered his gaze.

"Now, what were you meditating on, hmmm?"

"Did you know there is a song of the Betrothed?"

"The betrothed, a marriage song?"

Náidin shook his head. "Cyríon hid his Betrothed, and the Priests say someday she will return to us."

"So, they do more than just play music it seems."

"Aye, they keep the deepest secrets of our beginnings."

Náidin entered his father's workshop. The heat from the kilns and furnaces washed over him. His father worked at a grinding wheel. He lifted the arm above the disc and shut the valve to the water driving the gears.

"Welcome, son." Thalin waved him over.

Náidin hugged his father. "What would you have me start with?"

His father started him on a broach made from a single piece of wire.

Náidin plopped into his seat at the table. It felt good to be home. How many others apprenticed with their families? Meráda placed a heaping plate before him.

"Thank you, mother." He grinned and then breathed in the savory smell.

"What did you learn today?" She asked as she took her seat.

Náidin fished into his belt pouch and pulled out the twisted and hammered broach. "Here, Mother. It is for you."

She smiled and pinned it above her breast. "It is lovely."

"The boy has a good eye and a steady hand." Thalin clapped him on the shoulder.

A knock sounded on the door. "I'll get it." Náidin popped up and hurried to the door.

Kalidin hooked his arm in his and led him back to the table, kicking the door shut behind him.

"We should lock it." Náidin tried to turn back.

"You can lock it when I leave."

Náidin grabbed a setting for his brother and placed it before him as he settled in. "Father taught me to make a broach. What did your Master teach you?"

"Exercises to prepare me." Kalidin replied as he served himself from his brother's overfilled plate.

Meráda tsked as she passed a basket of rolls to Kalidin. "Such a vague answer."

"Did you leave a pack at the door?" Thalin scowled as he studied Kal. "Cyríon forbid if Náidin wanders off in the night to find you."

"I won't wander off." Náidin quipped around a mouthful of roast.

Kalidin punched his brother in the arm. "Swallow first."

"And that is no more acceptable at the table, Kalidin." Meráda chided.

"Sorry, Mother," they replied in unison.

"I will not be staying the night as he no longer needs me so close. The priests broke our bond and let it remake itself." Kalidin put on arm around Náidin. "And he knows I'm not to tell him what I am learning, yet he tries to pry anyway."

A loud rapping on the door reverberated through the house. Thalin glowered as he pushed to his feet. "What is all fired so urgent at this hour?"

Lord Gríson pushed around Thalin as they entered the dining room. "Highly irregular to have one's own children under your roof during their Ten Year. One would think you had already familiarized them with your trade, Thalin."

"Only Náidin is under my tutelage for his discovery time. His brother's Master allowed him a visit."

Gríson turned to Kalidin. "I was satisfied to leave you both where you started. However, it reached me you had stopped your time in the Temple. What trade do you explore?"

"One arranged by Master Láin." Kalidin bowed his head to their House Lord. "As I will not be pledging to the Temple, there is not much more they can teach me."

"I've been told you are both fair healers for your age, I ask you both to reconsider."

"I thought you wanted only me consigned to the Temple." Náidin scowled.

"Ah, but your brother in returning ruined the chance for an advantageous betrothal." Lord Gríson sneered. "I have no use for this branch to continue outside of my edicts."

Meráda stood. "You have vexed this family since I bore them. Why? What is so wrong in letting both twins live their lives?"

"It evidently proved a detriment to the Body of Cyríon. Letting an Avatar near once named destroyed it."

Náidin's skin crawled as Gríson glared at him. "The Priest who controlled them gave them more honor than you." He looked up at the Lord. "You call them 'it' as if they were one thing. The Nameless no longer exist in fear and pain."

"So the Priests tell me. They do not condemn you." He looked about the room. "Kalidin can continue whatever Master Láin set him. Náidin returns to the Temple for the duration of the Discovery Cycle."

"Cousin." Thalin placed a hand on Gríson's shoulder. "Let the lads finish their meal. Join us."

"He won't perish for lack of finishing one meal."

Náidin cast his eyes down and slid his chair out. "I will get my pack."

Náidin trudged behind Lord Gríson.

"I have arranged for you to sit with the Record Keepers." Gríson gestured at the door before him.

Náidin looked about. "This is separate from the rest?"

"It is. Master Láin coddles you too much." He held his hand out. "Here you will remain in silence; give me the drum."

He shook his head clutching it to his chest. "I am a Keeper of the Song, this is the instrument given me."

A dower priest stepped out the door. "This is the Avatar?"

"So the other priests have said." Lord Gríson shrugged. "I fear they are correct."

"You hate anything beyond your control."

"We are losing our ways." Gríson snapped.

A smirk appeared on the priest's face as he turned to Náidin. "I am Master Doryn. When you enter this door, you will remain silent."

He held even tighter to his drum.

Master Doryn chuckled. "Keep it, but you may not play it. Understood?"

Náidin swallowed hard and nodded. "Aye."

"You will read the histories. After each you will write your impressions."

"And if I have questions?"

"Write them down."

"I would rather he not keep the drum." Lord Gríson beckoned Náidin to hand it over.

"Gríson, old friend, it is not for you to separate a Keeper from his ordained instrument."

"I grow weary of my edicts on this member of my House being

ignored."

"Pray that Cyríon reminds you, that one entered into the Temple is no longer yours to command."

"He has taken no vows to my knowledge." Gríson narrowed his eyes. "In fact, he denies he will serve in the Temple."

"An Avatar never takes a vow. Now, Lord Gríson leave us, as what I need to instruct him in is not for your ears."

"Very well."

Náidin watched his House Lord stalk off.

"Let us not leave you standing out in the cold too long."

He turned to the priest. "Master Doryn, I don't belong here."

"No, however, I believe what you may write will be of value to our people."

Fat wet snowflakes began falling. Náidin wasn't sure what made him shudder more, the biting cold around him or the thought of having to spend weeks in the Quiet. He eyed the door.

"It is never easy for a Keeper to sit with us. In truth, I believe Lord Gríson intends this as punishment."

"I would believe it." Náidin shrugged. "It seems nothing I do meets with his approval."

"I have told you the most important of what you will do here. I expect you to remain silent until released, except when raising your voice in song and beating your drum. I will have you escorted for your morning meditation to the Keepers."

He couldn't help the smile that spread.

"Your soup grows cold in your cell." Master Doryn turned to enter the Silent Halls. "Come."

Náidin followed, shaking off the snow as he entered.

Náidin jumped at the sound of heavy volumes dropping on the table. He stifled a cough as the resulting dust tickled his throat. He looked up at the Librarian and raised an eyebrow.

The stern woman just smiled and walked away.

He finished writing his thoughts on the last Avatar's writings. Other than the silence, his time in the Quiet was not the punishment that Lord Gríson had intended. The first few days he had to suppress the urge to hum. He found himself acutely aware of the incidental sounds of life. Who knew being quite could be so noisy? By the end of the first week, he was able to ignore them.

He often found himself lost in the reading as his mind absorbed everything. He set what would be his initial contributions to the Library aside to dry and picked the first volume from the stack. The wood and leather-bound book had no marking on its spine or cover.

A journal then. He opened the cover and began reading. Caught up in the illustrations, maps, and words of the trader, he found himself quite stiff by the time he felt a hand on his shoulder.

He turned to see Master Doryn. He closed the volume he'd been reading. Náidin reached for his slate and scribbled a question. "Who's writing?"

The priest took the slate and wrote his reply. "Orláin, an orphan sent by the Temple to Apprentice with a trader."

Orláin. His eyes widened as he took it back. "He became Master Láin!"

Doryn smiled as he read the deduction and gave a short nod.

Náidin grinned as he followed the old priest to evening meal. Other than the cold soup his first night, the meals in the Quiet were communal. There was something reassuring in having the others about despite not being able to speak.

CHAPTER 15:
KALIDIN'S 8TH VERSE

K alidin made his way back to the dorm. Mistress Díja looked up from her tatting frame. "Welcome back, Kalidin."

"Are you sure?"

"Aye. No drum tucked under your arm."

Kalidin laughed. "Fair enough. Is my brother returned?"

Mistress Díja shook her head. "He will return late. Seems he found something he wanted to continue reading."

"Where would I find him?"

"In the Quiet, and no, you may not go seek him."

Kalidin's shoulders slumped and he leaned on the desk.

"He is never far from you." She motioned to a sideboard. "Pour us some tea and then sit with me."

Kalidin grabbed two cups and poured from the warmed pot. The hint of lavender wafted on the steam. He breathed deep, letting go of the disquiet he felt.

He brought the cups to Mistress Díja. "Might we go in your office?"

She marked her progress and rose to her feet. "Come along."

He placed the cups on her desk and sank into the chair.

"What is bothering you, Kalidin?"

He placed a bobbin of silk before her. "The fact I've been told learning such things may be necessary to keep Náidin safe when we leave here."

"That is one I was working with, when?"

"Right before you told me to get the tea." He bowed his head.

"May you never have to use such skills." She came around the desk and pulled him close.

Kalidin settled into his desk, the seat beside him still empty. He took out his journal and his essay on his Discovery Cycle. The others chatted around him. They'd given up the last two weeks trying to get him to talk with them.

"Náidin, take your seat."

His head snapped up at Master Láin's words. He smiled at this grinning twin. "About time."

Náidin grasped for something at his side and met air, then laughed. "Had something to finish."

Kalidin punched his twin in the shoulder as he sat down. He received a kick under the table in return.

"You have all finished your first Discovery Cycle. Now that Náidin has rejoined us, we will discuss your time exploring possible paths."

Lúc stood.

"What did you learn?" Master Láin asked.

"That nothing I tried interested me." He made a face causing the rest of the class to laugh.

"Did your choices include what you thought you might want to do?"

"Aye, now I don't know what I want to do." Lúc threw his hands up.

"Anyone else feel the same?"

Several dwarflings raised their hands.

"Did any of your choices lead you to a possible choice for the next cycle?"

"There were parts I liked about my first choice. I want to work with metal, but blacksmith is not for me."

"Seek our father, Thalin, next cycle. He is a jeweler." Kalidin offered.

"Kal and I won't be following in his craft, we are called elsewhere." Náidin continued.

Lúc nodded and sat down.

"Did any find their calling?"

Several nodded.

"How many will still explore other paths next cycle?

Most replied they would.

"It is good to keep your minds open. Though, there is no fault in being sure of what you want."

Kalidin stood.

"Yes?" Master Láin gestured.

"When you know that Náidin and I are set on our path and not given to choose what we studied, why did we need to wait for my brother?"

"Which of your experiences did you prefer?"

"Being given more responsibility with the healers." Kalidin stood taller.

"And your other studies, how do you feel about them?"

He shrugged. "I can see their use."

"And the reason we did wait, Náidin?" Master Láin asked.

Náidin stood. "I didn't care for the silence, but the reading was fascinating, especially your old journals."

Láin raised an eyebrow. "Soon will be the Blossom Festival, I am glad you were given those, as my Dreamings say you will leave us not long after."

Kalidin scowled.

"I wanted you both part of this so you know what it is to be part of the Earthen Folk. To understand the steps that bring you to your majority. You have both had your future thrust on you, true. The training you've undertaken has matured you beyond your years."

"Kalidin!" Mistress Díja called out.

He turned to see her beckoning him. "Mistress?" He queried as he approached.

"Where is your brother?" She asked as she tried to catch her breath.

"Would you believe in the Quiet looking up texts?"

"He'll want to see one of the outsiders that have come. She is giving a demonstration before the festival."

Kalidin looked to the flower garlands in his hands. "I would retrieve him..."

"But, you have a task assigned." She chuckled."And likely your brother's task as well."

"I don't mind. I love the sweet smell of these. My mother wears their oil."

"Continue. I'll retrieve him." She waved and hurried off.

Kalidin blinked back tears. "So, this is it." He mumbled to himself.

He took a deep breath and continued his task.

The smell of the bonfire reached his nose before he entered the clearing. Lord Gríson had thrown such a fit at the prospect of the outsiders being allowed in the Halls, especially to play music, so they set up outside.

Kalidin moved to the front half log and sat, leaving space for Náidin to join him. The clearing filled around him in anticipation. He could hear Náidin excusing himself as he pushed through those seeking a seat and smiled.

His twin slid on to the log beside him, his drum in hand. "Kal, do you think it is the one from my Dreamings?"

He bumped his brother with a shoulder. "Who else? Are you truly excited we'll be leaving all we know?"

Náidin's smile fell. "No, yes, I don't know. It is what we are meant for. I'll miss everyone."

Kalidin nodded.

"We'll return though."

He looked over at his brother. "You will. There are things said to me..."

"I wouldn't return without you." Náidin rolled his eyes.

"You may not have a choice."

CHAPTER 16:
NÁIDIN'S 8TH VERSE

Náidin felt his excitement evaporate. His brother's apprehension bothered him. He started to look at their friends around him. What future did they have? How long would they be gone?

He twisted even further, and he could see their parents at the back. He smiled and waved. Their mother waved back, his father nodded. He could see the glint of the brooch he made on their mother's cloak.

His attention returned to the space before him. A woman, reed-thin and tall by Earthen Folk standards stood before them a wooden instrument in her hand. "Thank you for allowing me to share my music with you. I am, Shenrei Zelna of Takahan, a bard."

"A blessing on your hearth, Shenrei!" Náidin called, which earned him a cuff to the back of his head from Kalidin. He rubbed his head and stuck his tongue out at his brother.

"And on yours." Shenrei laughed. "My companion, she gestured to a man, who towered over the Earthen Folk even seated, "is my husband Kohahl Zelna of Lysandra, a Ranger of the Free Traders and protector of Travelers."

"Pardon, Mistress Shenrei, what is the instrument you hold?" Náidin asked.

Nikta laughed. "Of course, Náidin would ask."

The woman smiled, and Náidin saw her gaze drop to his drum. "I was told other than a Lullaby and a song of Mourning there was no music in Akekelth, and why we are playing outside the Mountain Halls."

"There is in the Temple. I'm a Keeper of Cyríon's Song, though I do not pledge to the Order."

"This is a fiddle." She winked at him, placed it beneath her chin and drew the bow across the strings.

The lively tune she played reverberated through his whole being. He let the music move him and found its rhythm. Soon he joined her on his drum. Song after song they played together.

When the music ended, Náidin glanced at his brother. "I'm sorry, Kal, it seems this time I decide for you."

"I already knew." He sighed.

Náidin walked to Shenrei. "Mistress, Cyríon has set you on this path. I would learn from you."

"You're asking to be my apprentice?"

"Aye."

She looked past him. "Your twin doesn't seem so enthusiastic. Would you leave him?"

"He comes with." Náidin replied his head bowed.

"I can see taking on one, but not two."

Náidin felt Kal's hand on his shoulder. "Then perhaps your husband would take me as his?"

"Kohahl?" Shenrei queried.

"This may be the first we've been in Akekelth, but the two of you don't look to be finished with your Ten Year." He sauntered over and put an arm around Shenrei.

"It is our fifth year." Náidin offered.

"My brother is an Avatar of Cyríon. His Dreamings foretold this." Kalidin shrugged. "And I am his Guardian."

"As children of your people," Kohahl stated, "you will both need a guardian of another sort."

"We've known this was coming." Thalin replied as he walked up and placed a hand on his and his brother's shoulders. "Meráda and I give consent if you will take them."

"As if they wouldn't after Náidin's Dreamings led him to ask." Meráda sighed.

"Are you certain?" Kohahl asked their parents.

Shenrei looked at her husband. "From what I've learned in the other Clans, if the boy's Dreamings said he goes with us, then yes they are." She knelt in front of Náidin. "I am honored Cyríon has chosen me to mentor his Avatar."

"I'll accept the Avatar's Guardian as my apprentice." Kohahl placed a hand on Kalidin's shoulder.

"King Caidél will have to release them to your care." Meráda dabbed at tears.

"My esteemed cousin is not likely to bring it before him."

Náidin stood beside his brother in the throne room. King Caidél set his seal to the Writ of Guardianship. "Though these children of Nerhaed House are not orphaned, and you are not of the Earthen Folk, I remand them to your care."

"It has been discussed with the Temple and the both of you, and it is agreed given the differences in our people and the Dreamings that their apprenticeship cannot wait for them to complete their Ten Year."

"I accept the guardianship of both children, and Náidin, son of Thalin of Nerhaed House as my apprentice." Shenrei held her hand out, and King Caidél placed the Writ in her open hand.

Kohahl placed his over the Writ above Shenrei's. "I also accept the guardianship of both children, and take Kalidin, son of Thalin of Nerhaed House as my apprentice."

The staccato of Lord Gríson's footfalls sounded in the Throne Room.

"Forgive me, my tardiness. It is odd I was not informed to be present in Council on a matter regarding members of my House."

"They are Acolytes of the Temple, Lord Gríson" the King addressed their father's cousin. "And as Náidin follows his ordained path, it is the Temple's purview, rather than their House's."

"Headstrong child, watch him Mistress," Lord Gríson spat. "However, Kalidin, I can see the longing to stay in you, yet you follow your brother's folly regardless. The trades you take..." He shook his head. "You are both Sanctioned. You have both chosen paths not of our people; it is best you never return."

They watched Lord Gríson stalk out the door. Náidin bowed his head. "I'm sorry, Kal."

"Don't be."

The King placed a hand on each of their heads. "He can refuse to represent you in Council; however, that is as far as he can sanction you. He will likely move to formerly exile the both of you. I will not allow it."

"We are grateful," Náidin replied.

"With the Festival done and to avoid further trouble, you should both say your farewells so we may leave," Shenrei suggested.

Náidin sat his new pony his brother on another beside him. He looked over at Kal to see him turned in his saddle as their home disappeared, obscured by the forest.

"Just think of the visions we had in the Light Room! To see those for ourselves." Náidin grinned.

"Bet by tonight, you won't be so cheerful." Kalidin shook his head.

"Considering how my backside is already aching from the saddle, I agree."

So began their journey into the wider world.

ABOUT THE AUTHOR

J'nae Rae Spano is originally from Portland, Oregon. She lives with her husband, Chris, in Lemon Grove, California. She has a passion for the arts in most of its forms and is active in Science Fiction Fandom. She currently does Programming for ConDor, San Diego's longest running SF/F convention.

Also by J'nae Rae Spano

Flash Fiction

The Trade's On, Published in Sci Phi Journal #8

Nine-Tenths. Published on Empyreome.com-Daily Flash Fiction

Books

Náidin's Song Cycle:

Náidin's Song: Blood Bound

Náidin's Song: Twins

Watch for more stories in the Náidin's Song Cycle

Dragon Kin Chronicals

Cocky Dragon Slayer